DELIVERING DREAMS

LORI PREUSCH

Established in 1983
Exclusive publisher of all artwork by Lori Preusch
P O Box 4030
Durango, Colorado 81302
www.dandelionpress.com

My heart-felt thanks to everyone who so graciously contributed to this project offering
unwavering support, guidance and encouragement. And my sincere and deepest gratitude to
all of you who have purchased my paintings, prints and cards from as far back as 1983. It is
you who have opened a window to my creativity, to my art and to my life.

The illustrations in this book were painted in acrylic on canvas.
Book and jacket design by Lori Preusch.
Jacket copy written by Michelle Martino.
The text was set in Deepdene.
Printed in China by Four Colour Print Group Louisville, Kentucky

First Edition

Library of Congress Control Number:
2016931629

Summary: Inspired by her adventurous Grandpa's letters, a young girl embarks on a magical,
imaginative journey around the world.

ISBN 978-0-692-52818-1

FOR STEPHEN AND CAMERON
DREAMS DELIVERED

My mailbox, the color of white winter light, silently stands through the day and the night.

It looks over the hill that I climb every day,
one thousand and two smiling footsteps away.

Together we're still like the shadows in grass,
as we silently wait for the postman to pass.

Cloud shadows sail on a soft grassy sea,
whispering as they roll by, "Come with me …"

I cheered with delight to the listening sky,
the day that the postman finally stopped by.
A letter from Grandpa laid gently for me,
told tales of adventure and traveling free.

My Grandpa he writes of a wide open world,
of places he's seen and adventures unfurled:
Silvery snow on a clear polar night,
lazy safaris and Turkish delight.

Aried Feb 27. gk.

AIR MAIL

OCT 28
U.S.
4 3 P
VIA AIR MAIL
POSTAGE
8¢

OCT 28
43CPM
1938

He writes of his treks through Nepal on a yak,
and swimming with dolphins, the sun on their backs.
Of pyramids lost in the vast golden sand,
where traveling merchants have treasures in hand.
Of people in Venice who wear hats and bright stripes,
and a place called Bombay where the mangoes are ripe.
Vast misty moorlands and old, sleepy bogs,
and tropical canopies hidden by fog.
Deep, cobalt pools where mourning doves croon,
where silence and secrets roll in with the moon.

I run to deliver my urgent reply,
through dapples of sunlight and grey cotton sky.

"Oh Grandpa, send letters to me every day,
of every adventure you have on your way!"

I never thought that a mailbox was more,
than a plain dusty box with a squeaky tin door.
But that rusty old mailbox helped me discover,
I'm connected to everywhere one way or another.

"Attention all letters that I have collected-
sweep me away to the vast unexpected!"
Typefaced, d o u b l e   s p a c e d and even UPPER CASE,
my mailbox sends me exploring posthaste.

I don't have an inkling of what I might find,
as I rush out to greet that old mailbox of mine.
That squeaky-hinged door of shiny old tin,
is an airplane that flies like an apron on wind.
"Higher and higher!" I shout to the breeze,
over a patchwork of fields stitched with trees.

Each day now behind that gleaming tin door,
are letters to dream in and words to explore.
I've lassoed my dreams. I am ready and dressed,
to go and explore the American West.
Hair loose at both ends flying wild and free
on a breath of fresh air, you'll never catch me.

My mailbox and I have cast off once again,
to sail our dream like the wandering wind.
I'm friends with the seagulls who often drop by,
to bring their reports of the tropical sky.
They lead us to islands of pastel and gold,
where glistening days overlap and unfold.

We ride on the range where it's quiet and still,
far, far away from my little green hill.
The road uncoils like a long, amber thread,
as Grandpa's words beckon us on ahead.

When darkness steps out, the nighttime is ours,
in a silent procession of deep, moody stars.
My mailbox, glowing a silvery blue,
delivers good dreams to me all the night through.

Then one day, behind that old mailbox door,
sat a letter I'd sent nearly five days before.
I looked for an answer. I read and reread,
a note from the postman that formally said,
"RETURN TO SENDER. We just couldn't find,
that Grandpa of yours anywhere at this time."

No letters to dream of or worlds to explore.
No fields of patchwork or far away shores.
Days and weeks passed with no letter in sight,
the hours dragged by like a long Arctic night.
No daydreams were left for my mailbox and me.
"Grandpa, oh where in the world could you be?"

a
30

b

70

c

60

I climbed up that hill, like one thousand steep stairs,
to look for the letter that never was there,
and found just a spider who'd moved in to stay.
But just as I turned to go walking away,
I caught a slight glint and I saw a reflection.
A letter arrived from the oddest direction.

d
40

e
20

f

o

g
20

h
40

k
70

l

120 Q 140 R 160 S 180 T 160 U 180 V 60 N 80 O 100 P 120 Q 140 R 160 S 180
a 80 b 70 c 60 d 40 e 20 f 0 g 20 h 40 k 70 l
P 120 Q 140 R 160 Q 140 T 160 U 180 V M 60 N 80 O 100 P 120 Q 140 R 160 S 180

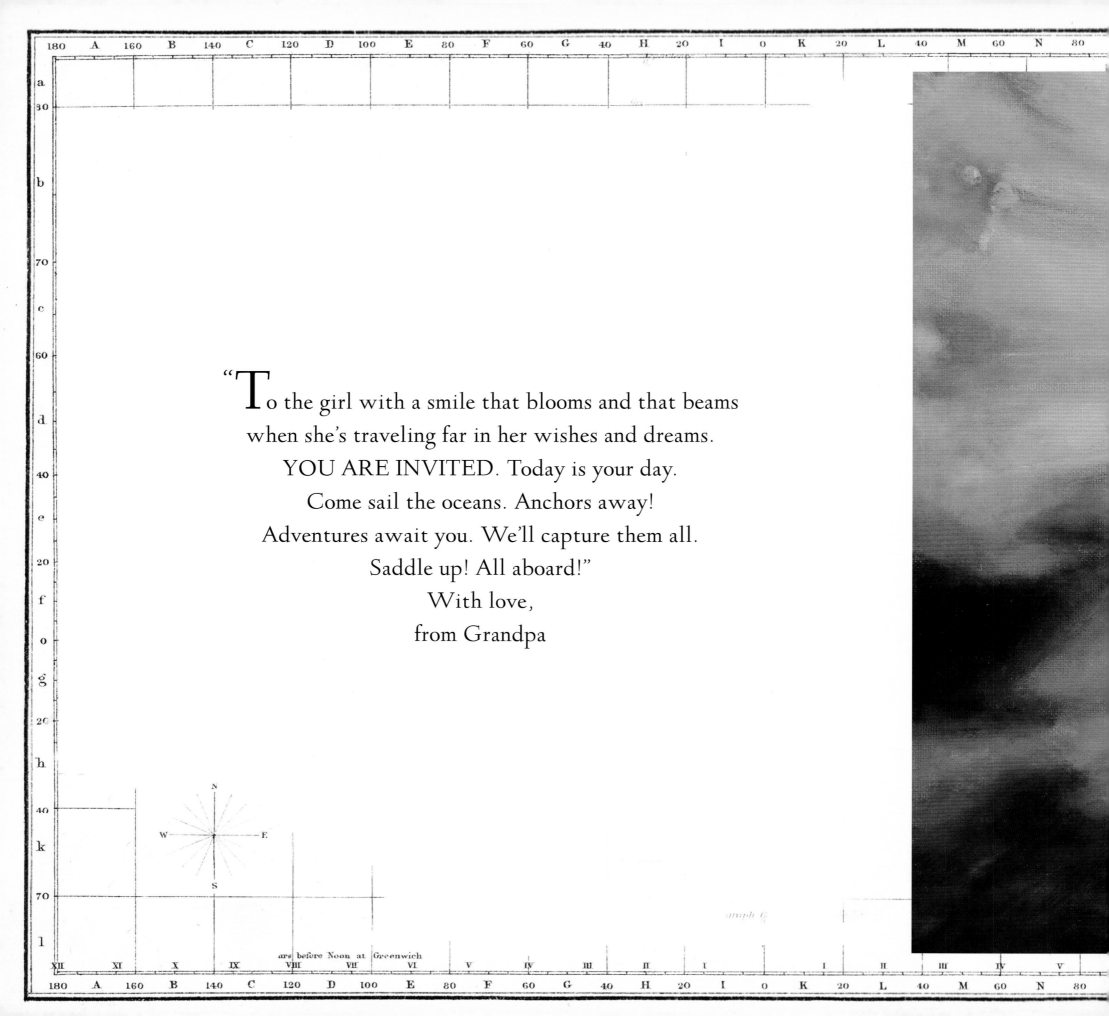

"To the girl with a smile that blooms and that beams
when she's traveling far in her wishes and dreams.
YOU ARE INVITED. Today is your day.
Come sail the oceans. Anchors away!
Adventures await you. We'll capture them all.
Saddle up! All aboard!"
With love,
from Grandpa

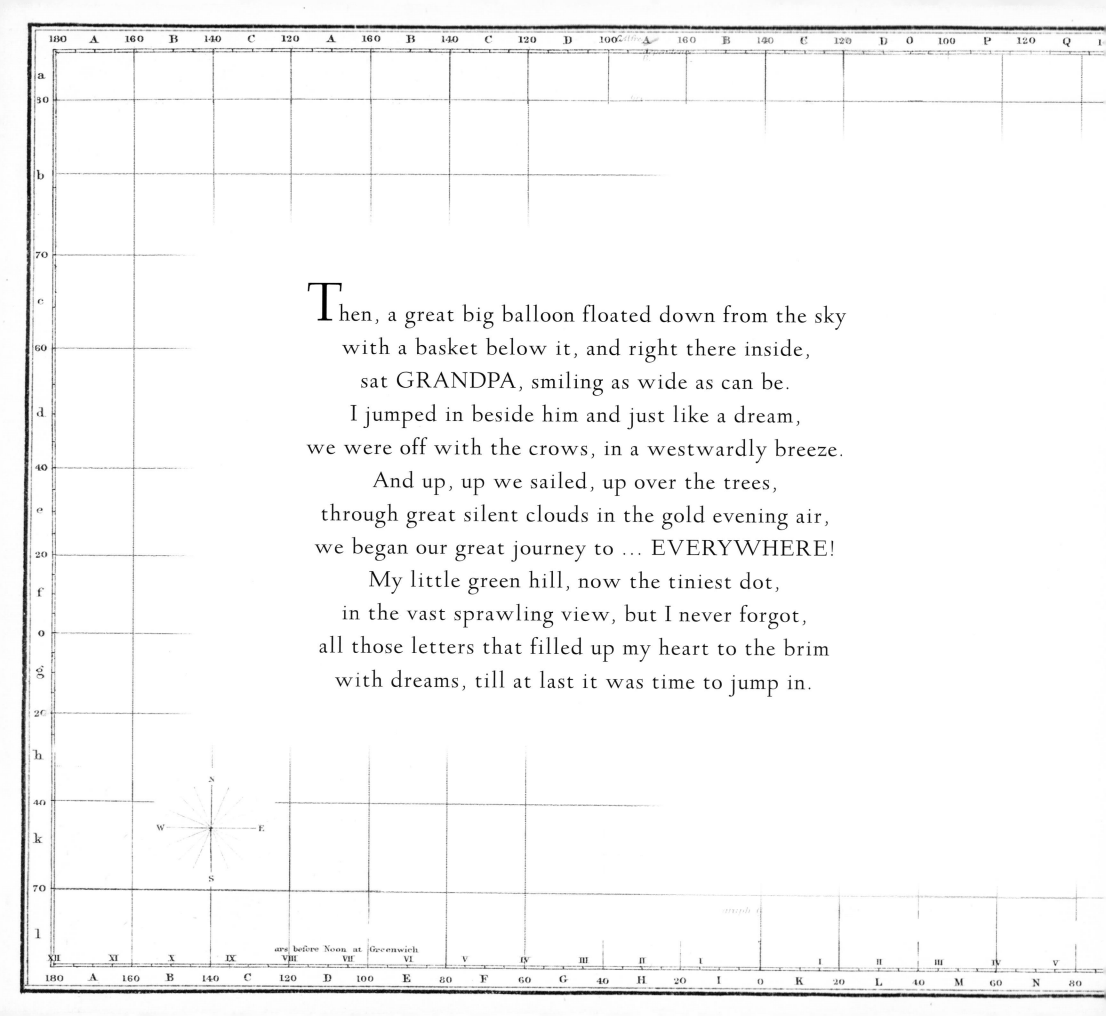

Then, a great big balloon floated down from the sky
with a basket below it, and right there inside,
sat GRANDPA, smiling as wide as can be.
I jumped in beside him and just like a dream,
we were off with the crows, in a westwardly breeze.
And up, up we sailed, up over the trees,
through great silent clouds in the gold evening air,
we began our great journey to … EVERYWHERE!
My little green hill, now the tiniest dot,
in the vast sprawling view, but I never forgot,
all those letters that filled up my heart to the brim
with dreams, till at last it was time to jump in.

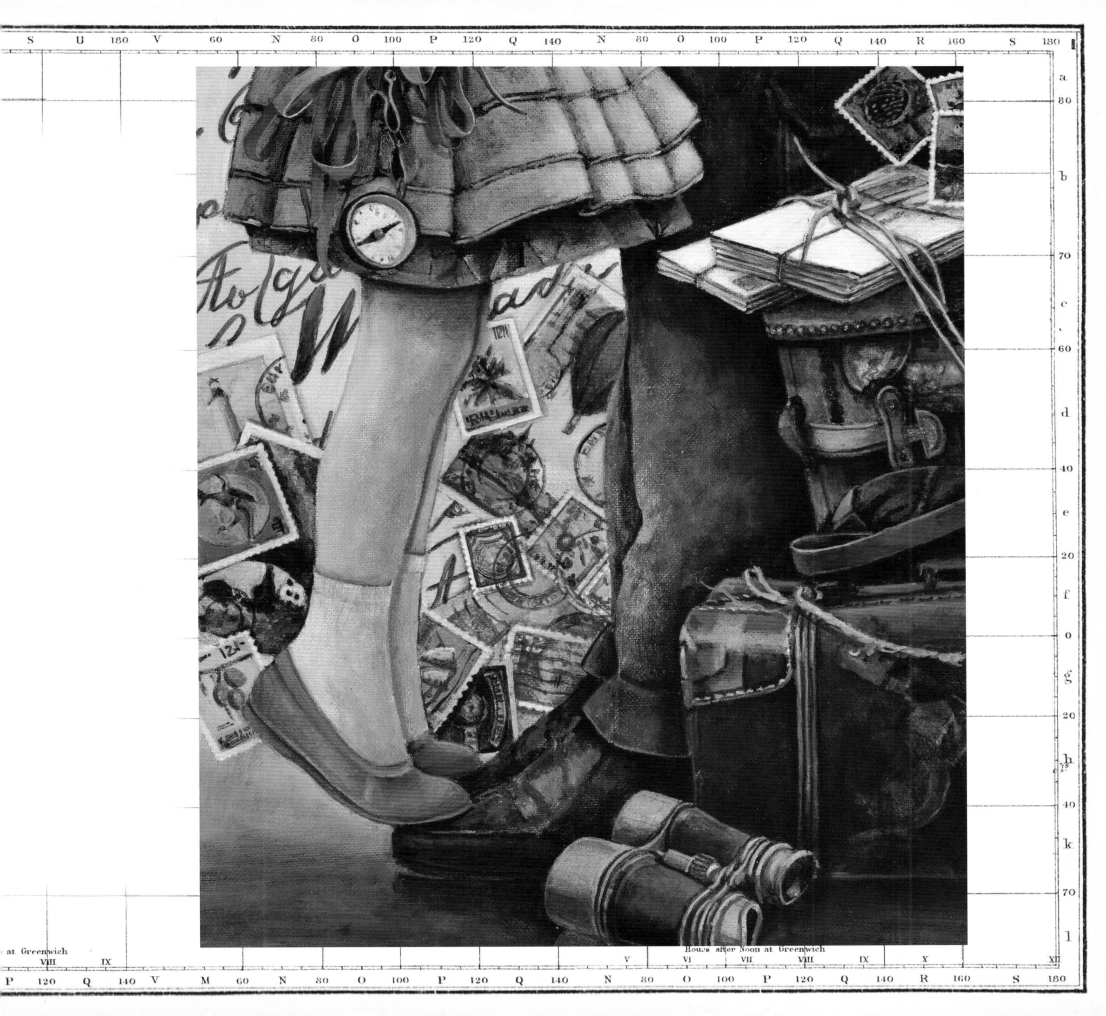

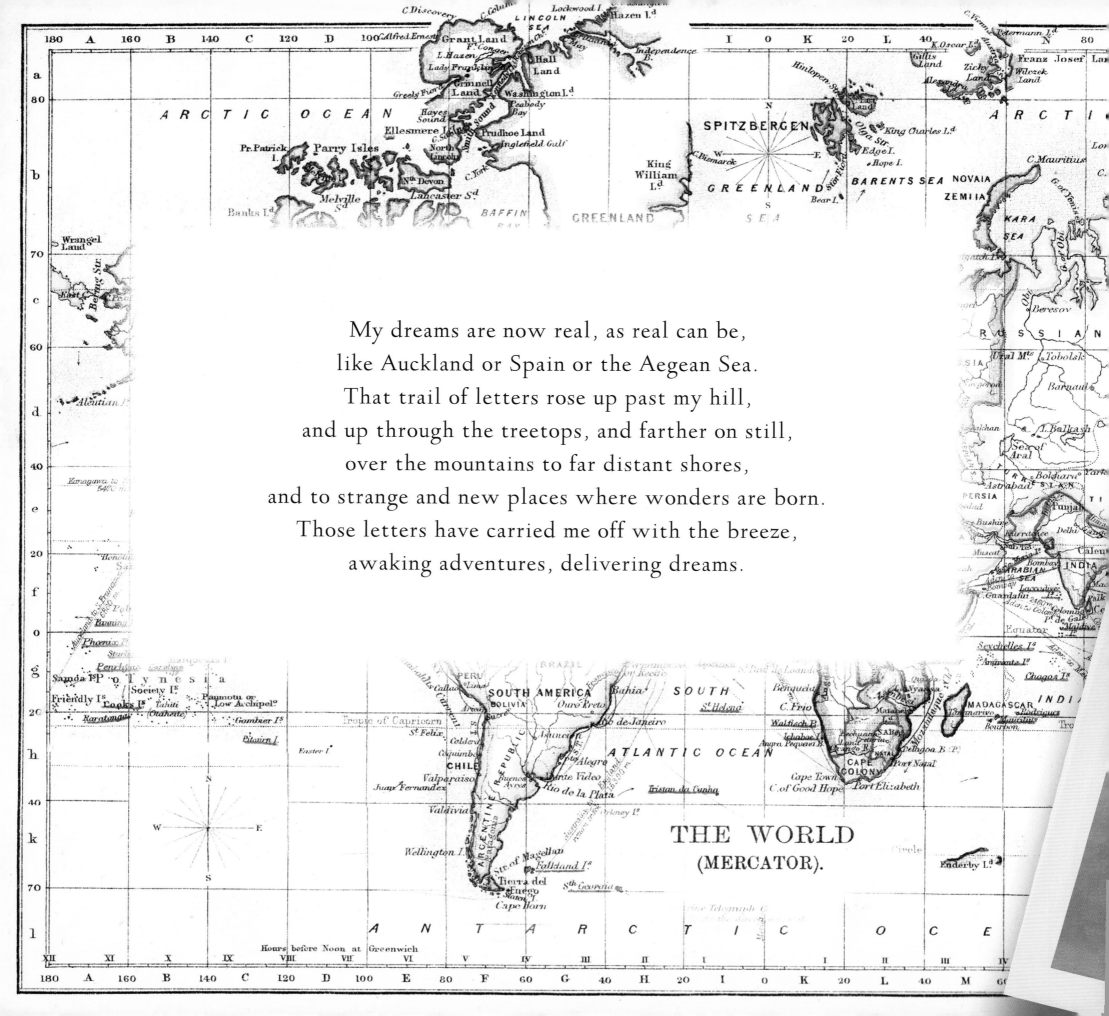

My dreams are now real, as real can be,
like Auckland or Spain or the Aegean Sea.
That trail of letters rose up past my hill,
and up through the treetops, and farther on still,
over the mountains to far distant shores,
and to strange and new places where wonders are born.
Those letters have carried me off with the breeze,
awaking adventures, delivering dreams.

"THE WORLD IS BUT A CANVAS TO OUR IMAGINATION."

-THOREAU